Sam Wood

Random Rhymes

Sam Wood

Random Rhymes

ISBN/EAN: 9783337387310

Printed in Europe, USA, Canada, Australia, Japan

Cover: Foto ©Andreas Hilbeck / pixelio.de

More available books at **www.hansebooks.com**

RANDOM RHYMES.

BY

SAM WOOD.

BARNSLEY :

W. R. MASSIE, 3, Market Hill.

1896.

This small Volume

is most respectfully dedicated to

NORMAN GALE.

For permission to republish the greater number of these Rhymes the author's thanks are due to the proprietors of *Old and Young*, and of *Chambers's Journal*.

CONTENTS.

CONTENTS—*Continued.*

No academic lore I bring,
   No philosophic preaching;
In simple strains I simply sing
   The songs of Nature's teaching.

S. W.

A PASTORAL

BENEATH the April sky
The sorrel buds are peeping,
And vernal blades are creeping
    Through grasses dead and dry.
    The speedwell's deep-blue eye
Toward the sun is glancing,
And the brook is merrily dancing
O'er pebbled places shallow,
    And the pewit's startling cry
Floats o'er the weedy fallow,
    Beneath the April sky.

Bathed by the April rain,
The greener fields are gleaming,
And water-flags are streaming
    By lake and mere again.
    On either side the lane
The birds are blithely singing,
And the lark its flight is winging
Into the trackless azure ;
    And where dead leaves have lain,
Sweet Flora spreads her treasure,
    Bathed by the April rain.

Amid the April glow,
Young Phyllis seeks the meadows,
And 'neath the dappled shadows
    She hears the freshet flow.
    Soft winds that lightly blow
Do wanton with her tresses,
While the shepherd boy's caresses
She blushingly receiveth ;
    And the westering sun is low
Or ere his side she leaveth,
    Amid the April glow.

DISCONTENT.

I MAY not live content :
   The thornless paths of life,
   The years that know not strife,
For me were never meant.

Give me a goal to gain ;
   The racer's keen delight ;
   A worthy prize in sight,
And space across the plain.

Let me pursue my quest,
   With Hope, my guide, before ;
   For when the race is o'er
There's time enough to rest.

Toil its own blessing brings ;
   So while I live be mine
   The discontent divine
That leads to nobler things.

A REQUEST.

LET us be friends : we may not now be more ;
   Your silent glances make but poor amends
For all my pain.   If nought will love restore,
   Let us be *friends*.

Love to my heart its fire no longer lends ;
   'Tis chilled and hardened to its very core :
No quickening beat your presence now attends.

Yet would I not forget the joys of yore ;
   And now that Fate has worked its cruel ends,
Shake hands and smile ; for my sake, I implore,
   Let us be friends.

A SONG OF THE WORK-A-DAY WORLD.

In this work-a-day world there is sadness ;
　　There is sorrow enough and to spare ;
There is heart-ache and grief for the mother,
　　And each child has its portion of care.
　　Oh, we all have our burdens to bear ;
　For the rich there are worries and losses,
　For the poor there are trials and crosses ;
　　So let us take bravely our share,
And do what we can for each other.
　　For we mostly get measure for measure,
　　　And the loss often equals the gain,
　　So the rich do not get all the pleasure,
　　　And the poor do not get all the pain.

In this work-a-day world there is gladness :
　　There is music and sunshine for all :
There are joys of her own for the mother,
　　And childhood is sweet on the whole.
　　Unto each shall some pleasure befall :
　For the rich there are fortunes and fashions,
　For the poor there are love-prompted passions ;
　　So let us be hopeful of soul,
And rejoice on our way with each other.
　　For we mostly get measure for measure,
　　　And the loss often equals the gain,
　　So the rich do not get all the pleasure,
　　　And the poor do not get all the pain.

MATING SONG.

A BONNIE bird sang on a hawthorn spray,
   "Come, little sweetheart, come;"
He warbled his love in a melting lay;
   "Come, let us build a home.
We'll make us a nest 'mid the leaves and flowers,
Where the shade and the scent shall alike be ours;
We'll flutter around when the sun shines bright,
And rest in the hedge through the starlit night;
We'll hie through the fields at the peep of dawn,
And gather the worms when the meads are mown
And when thou shalt sit on the burdened nest,
I'll sing thee my sweetest of songs, and best;
And when the young birdies shall need our care
Together we'll gather the daily fare."
So the little bird warbled through sunlit hours,
But he gave not a thought to the storms and showers.

A bonnie lad waited beside a stile:
   "Come, little sweetheart, come;"
He thought of a maiden and sang the while,
   "Come, let us build a home.
We'll rear us a cot on a breezy hill,
And sit out of doors when the winds are still;
We'll trip to the market, the fête, and fair,
And barter or dance with the youngest there;
We'll rise to our work when the morning calls,
·And walk in the fields when the twilight falls;
And when in the cradle thy babe shall lie,
I'll toil whilst thou tend'st it with watchful eye;
Together we'll walk through the ways of life,
And our home shall be happy and free from strife."
And so, when his sweetheart came that way,
He spoke not a word of "a rainy day."
And 'tis well for the bird and well for the boy
When they harbour no thought that would mar their joy.

TAKE CARE.
(FOR A PICTURE).

TAKE care, indeed ! Oh, heart, my heart, take care !
  Was ever smile so arch or face so sweet ?
Did ever Cupid glance from orbs so fair ?
  Or, glancing, gain a conquest more complete ?

O woman ! thou art master evermore ! ·
  To win thy smile all mortal ills we brave.
Men woo or worship, lure, entreat, implore ;
  For man is evermore thy willing slave.

TO THE FIRST CELANDINE.

ERE the sweet thrush attuned its speckled throat,
  Or ere the blackbird's thrilling song was heard,
My eager glance thy golden petals caught,
      And I was strangely stirred.

The buds upon the thorn were scarcely seen,
  Nor had the fluttering lark essayed to sing,
When thou appeared'st amid the quickening green,
      A solitary thing.

Lured into bloom by one brief sunny day,
  Thy fleeting life, alas, must soon be o'er ;
But 'tis thy honoured lot to lead the way
      For countless millions more.

Thou art the herald of a lovely race ;
  But though 'tis thine to die ere storms are stilled,
Thou mayest depart contented from thy place,
      Thy mission all fulfilled.

Thou canst not live to see the spring unfold ;
  Nor view the glory of a vernal day ;
Thou canst not linger, blooming, to behold
      The crowning wealth of May.

Yet thine is but the lot of such as lead
  Onward to glorious periods, alone,
Of such as in the battle fight and bleed,
      And die at victory's dawn.

A WILD NIGHT.

SHRIEK, winds, shriek ;
Howl in your maddening flight o'er the desolate moor,
Moan through the pine trees, and wail by the cottager's door,
Bend the tall sunflowers low till they break ;
Shriek, winds, shriek !

Beat, rain, beat ;
Fall in fast drops all aslant on the wet window-pane,
Drench the brown kivers, and batter the still growing grain,
Soak through the bound sheaves of barley and wheat :
Beat, rain, beat !

Droop, clouds, droop ;
Trail your dark garments o'er woodland and hollow and hill,
Shut out the stars, and the sky with your black vapours fill,
Frown at the shepherd as lower ye swoop ;
Droop, clouds, droop !

WHEN FIRST WE MET.

(A ROUNDEL).

WHEN first we met, I thought you fair
Beyond all I had looked on yet ;
You came with such a winsome air
When first we met.
I shall not readily forget
Your glance, your smile, your voice so rare,
Your lustrous eyes of living jet.

But soon you stood revealed, and there
I saw a conquering coquette :
Ah, would that I had been aware
When first we met !

BALLADE OF LIFE'S SALT.

BRIGHT eyes are more than jewels rare,
  And looks are more than words, we know ;
And he who prizes what is fair,
  To seek it out is seldom slow ;
  Though gold its tempting weight may throw,
To turn the balance in the strife,
  Great Mammon rules not all below,
For Love is still the salt of life.

Young beauty never need despair,
  Nor grace or goodness yield to woe,
For who are they who will not dare,
  In spite of all, their choice to show ?
  True hearts in true affection grow,
And though rude scandal's tongue be rife,
  The gossips reap not all they sow,
For Love is still the salt of life.

Oh, precious antidote of care
  That sets heart-fountains all aflow !
How sadly should we mortals fare
  But for thy tender-passionate glow !
  Thy seasoning to each breast bestow,
Make savoury all this earthly strife,
  Be kind alike to high and low—
For Love is still the salt of life.

ENVOY.

Ah, Prince, mankind shall ever bow
  To sweetheart, mistress, maid, or wife
And love, while seasons come and go,
For Love is still the salt of life.

TO A BUTTERFLY.

Airy creature, frail and fair,
   Flitting o'er my garden bower,
Sailing lightly through the air,
   Like a floating flower.

Take to-day thy fill of life,
   'Mid the glory that remains ;
Revel where the scents are rife,
   Ere the sunlight wanes.

All the season's sweets are thine ;
   All for thee the roses blow ;
But when summer days decline
   Thou wilt haste to go.

Birds that springtide hours beguile
   With their gladly warbled lays,
Oft, outliving summer's smile,
   Pine through winter days.

Bees that by their labour live,
   Late and early on the wing,
(Each a patient fugitive)
   Hide away till spring.

Some like these would linger on :
   I would be a butterfly,
And when summer joys are gone,
   Creep away to die.

SERENADE.

Summer again, and roses,
  And twilight lingering late ;
The sound of reaping, and keen scythes sweeping,
  But still I wait, and wait.

Sweetheart, how long, I wonder,
  How long shall I woo in vain ;
I was thy lover ere May was over,
  And May has been again.

Lilac has bloomed, and hawthorn,
  And cherries are red on the tree ;
The birds have mated, but I have waited—
  How long must I wait—for thee ?

ROUNDEL.

She comes and goes along the street,
  Unconscious of my joys and woes.
Twice ev'ry day, and twice we meet.
    She comes and goes.
  Sometimes I wonder if she knows
How quick my startled pulses beat,
  When she with plain politeness bows.

And yet what matter how we greet,
  While love or romance round her throws
A glamour, as, with youthful feet,
    She comes and goes.

THE RUSTIC BRIDGE.

Some three fields distant from the village street,
A rustic footbridge spans the meadow brook,
Screened by tall hawthorn boughs on either bank,

Thither with lingering steps when dusk appears,
Or when the moon her silvery lamp uplifts,
Some amorous pair will wander arm in arm.

Full fifty years that rustic bridge hath stood,
And men whose heads are grey or in the grave,
There wooed the virgin playmates of their youth.

Since then each year hath brought some younger face
To linger there and lean above the brook,
Making a Venus' mirror of its depths.

What souls with love's whole rapture all aflame,
What hearts in youth's strong flood-tide throbbing warm,
Have found their first great joy while lingering here !

So, if this bridge had but the power of speech
To tell the story of its many scenes,
What passionate volumes here might be revealed !

Yet, often as I pass this sacred spot,
At morn or noon, but most in twilight hours,
Something of all this history there I glean.

AN AGREEABLE TEST.

WHEN I met her last night, with a rose in her hair,
  My eyes were bewitched by so charming a sight.
The rose with its wearer did poorly compare,
      When I met her last night.
She seemed such a merry-eyed, light-footed sprite,
So bewitchingly sweet, so enchantingly fair,
  That I could not believe her mortality quite :
So, just to be certain if mortal she were,
  And lest she should hastily vanish in flight,
I ventured to kiss her while no one was there,
      When I met her last night.

A VISION OF JOY.

ONE day I wandered, sad at heart
    For faults and failings all my own ;
    Dark shadows o'er my thoughts were thrown ;
Life had no comfort to impart.

Still brooding thus I sauntered on,
    When of a sudden I espied
    A smiling vision at my side :
One glance, and lo ! my gloom was gone.

It was a girl with laughing face,
    And sparkling eyes undimmed by care ;
    A joyous spirit good and fair,
A sprightly creature full of grace.

A flower, a picture, music, gold,
    Might thus for joy have made me glad,
    But when my heart again is sad
May I that sunny girl behold.

NIGHT AND TEMPEST.

HARK ! 'tis the trample of legions,
The rush of mad armies aerial through darkness and night,
Hear you the tumult, the clamour, the shriek of the troops in their
  flight,
  As they tear through the storm-beaten regions !

Hear you the sound of their moaning,
The heart-searching wail of each tortured, tempestuous voice ;
Hear you the rage and the fury, the thud and the boisterous noise,
  The sound of their sobbing and groaning !

Now in the night-battle meeting
The thick clouds loom upward all massive and frowning and black,
But the fierce tempest takes them and scatters them over its track,
  Abroad all the rain-torrents beating.

The black waters foam on the river,
The stoutest tree bends to the blast, and the tall chimneys rock ;
The cottage walls tremble, and palaces shake with the shock,
  Beasts crouch, and the shelterless shiver.

A WAYSIDE THOUGHT.

WHILE hastening home one drizzly winter day,
I saw a troop of children quitting school,
And as they tripped along the miry street,
Pleased with the freedom of the noontide hour,
Some ran with reckless feet into the mud,
Unmindful of bespattered clothes and shoes :
But others, stepping with all care, passed on
With undisfigured feet and garments clean.
'Tis thus, thought I, when wayward youth breaks loose
From the restraint of elder guardian hands ;
Some plunge with careless feet into life's path,
Where vice, like mire, lies deep along the way,
And stain their lives in the vile element ;
While others, heedful how and where they tread.
Walk on in spotless purity of soul.

I CANNOT GUESS.

(A ROUNDEL).

I CANNOT guess what Jennie thought
    When for a kiss I first did press :
If love a sudden rapture wrought,
        I cannot guess.

She seemed not full of wantonness,
    As would a maid by Love untaught :
Nor gave she token of distress.

I know she granted what I sought ;
    But if she loved me more or less,
Or held it sacred as she ought,
        I cannot guess.

MEADOW TREASURES.

ᴀʟʟ along the meadow ways
   There are treasures growing ;
Some with living gold ablaze,
   Some like rubies glowing.

Pearly daisies ' crimson-tipped ; '
   King-cups leaning over ;
Gleaming gorse-bloom, golden-lipped ;
   Rings of scarlet clover.

Blushing poppies shyly bent
   'Mid the long wheat lances ;
Agate bean-flowers rich with scent ;
   Speedwell's sapphire glances.

Milkmaids of the marshes born ;
   Stately ox-eyed daisies ;
Golden clouds amid the corn,
   Wrought of sharlock mazes.

Open roses on the brier,
   Matchless tints revealing ;
Broom with blossom all afire,
   Harebell buds concealing.

Woodbine chalices that rear,
   Curled in airy lightness ;
Spreading elder boughs that wear
   Bloom of snowy whiteness.

These are spread throughout the land,
   Free for every comer,
Scattered by the stintless hand
   Of our regal Summer.

WET WEATHER.

Fall, rain, fall :
Beat down all aslant on the gable and window and door,
Drench the lone herdsman and drive through the roofs of the poor,
    Trickle down rudely-built ceiling and wall ;
        Fall, rain, fall.

Blow, wind, blow :
Bend the tall poplars, and scatter the lingering leaves,
Strip the oak branches, and beat down the outlying sheaves :
    Whistle by panel and pane as you go ;
        Blow, wind, blow.

Flee, clouds, flee :
From the gate of the sunset let all your dark armies uptroop ;
Trail low o'er the moor ; like a pall o'er the wide valley droop :
    Silently tramp on your march o'er the sea ;
        Flee, clouds, flee.

Fade, flowers, fade :
Like the beautiful bow that is seen for awhile in the sky,
Like summer itself, like all that is destined to die,
    Sadly from meadow and garden and glade,
        Fade, flowers, fade.

I LONG TO REST

(A ROUNDEL).

I LONG to rest within thy virgin arm,
  O thou whom I have longest loved and best
Encompassed by thy silent, soothing charm,
      I long to rest.
  How have I waited with a lover's zest
For thy soft kiss, thy soul-refreshing balm,
  Yearning to lay my head upon thy breast !
Come, free my brain from fears and thoughts of harm,
  And let me be of those whom thou hast blessed :
Grant me again, O gentle Sleep, thy calm ;
      I long to rest.

THE LOVERS' HOUR.

Now evening wanes along the darkening west,
  Where lingers yet an afterglow of light,
  And slowly now the curtains of the night
Fall over fields where weary creatures rest ;
Dusk-loving moths the hedge-lined lanes infest ;
  Night-roving birds begin their ghostly flight ;
  The silent trees are fading out of sight,
And lagging teamsters trudge their homeward quest.

Now, while I wait a fairy form to greet,
  A welcome footfall on my hearing steals ;
The moon—its silvery crescent westward bowed—
Sails suddenly from out yond breaking cloud,
  And straightway to my waiting eyes reveals
A girlish face angelically sweet.

THE BROOK.

LAUGHING brooklet seaward flowing,
Under bridge and over boulder,
Let me lean my ear and listen
To thy ceaseless soothing treble ;
Softer than the rarest music
Ever made by moving fingers ;
Ever dropped in liquid sweetness
From the strings of harp or viol.
Let me hearken to thy gurgle,
Still monotonous and changeful ;
Tender as a lover's whisper,
Pleasant as an infant's laughter,
Breaking forth in joyous ripples.
Let me hear each fleeting cadence
Of thy waters bubbling, dripping ;
So may I each accent gather,
And repeat thy subtle singing.

BALLADE OF A SILENT SONGSTER.

Upon the dreamy mid-June night
　　There falls a spell of sweet content,　'
A rare, half-languorous delight,
　　With yearning love's fruition blent ;
　　Where late a flood of song had vent,
The twilit woods no longer ring ;
　　The springtide's rapturous thrill is spent,
The nightingale hath ceased to sing.

Young May, that fair, impassioned sprite,
　　Who came with colour, song, and scent,
Hath taken, all too soon, her flight,
　　And left us glories to lament ;
　　We're fain to follow where she went,
To track the footsteps of the spring,
　　For June the flood of song hath pent ;
The nightingale hath ceased to sing.

We linger in the lingering light.
　　Upon the twilit scene intent,
Scarce conscious of the long respite
　　From passion's fever and ferment ;
　　Nor do we mind the calmness lent,
For still to May our longings cling ;
　　We miss the strains magnificent
The nightingale hath ceased to sing.

ENVOY.

Ah, Prince, though other joys are sent,
　　Though passing days new pleasure bring,
We still regret the joy that went :
　　The nightingale hath ceased to sing.

" LA MASCOT."

LAUGHTER lights her ev'ry feature,
    And her eyes ;
She's the sweetest little creature
    'Neath the skies ;
From the hour that she arises,
She is full of glad surprises,
Full of guesses and surmises
    All so wise.

People listen for the patter
    Of her feet,
As they pause to hear her chatter
    In the street ;
She's the queen of all the city,
She's so charming and so witty.
So bewitching, and so pretty.
    And so sweet.

In her play and her apparel
    She is fair,
And you never hear her quarrel
    Anywhere ;
She'll be just the same to-morrow,
Free from malice, fret, and sorrow,
For she never seems to borrow
    Any care.

A SONG IN SUMMER.

SUNSHINE and roses around me,
 The song of the lark on high,
  The full completeness
  Of summer sweetness,
 The glory of earth and sky ;

Love, and the thrill of passion,
 The throbbing of pulses strong,
  The potent graces
  Of maiden faces ;
 A place in the lusty throng—

These are mine, and I know them
 To me through the summer lent ;
  I own a measure
  Of rarest pleasure,
 And I am all content.

So, when the summer waneth,
 And chill winds work their will,
  When songs are banished,
  And flowers have vanished,
 Give me contentment still.

––––––

A ROUNDEL.

How shall we meet when home again I turn
 After these years ? If, on the homeward street,
I suddenly her long-missed face discern,
  How shall we meet ?
Will she shake hands with common unconcern ?
 Or will she smile as glad my smile to greet ?
While tender blushes on her fair cheeks burn.

I wonder will her looks be sad or sweet,
 And will she speak the words for which I yearn ?
A thousand times this query I repeat,
  How shall we meet ?

GLOZE ROYAL.

They sin who tell us love can die....
  In heaven ambition cannot dwell....
With life all other passions fly....
  But Love is indestructible.—Southey

LUST but liveth for a day ;
Only brief is pleasure's stay :
  Who shall long on these rely ?
They have no affinity
With the sacred things that be,
  Wholly in the flesh they lie.
Love, whose power the soul sustains,
Lives through changes, fears, and pains :
  Though born, it may be, with a sigh,
  " *They sin who tell us love can die.*"

Hate is like the scattered spray,
When the winds around it play.
  Avarice points the way to hell,
Love is like a boundless sea,
Rolling on eternally ;
  Deep, but none its depth may tell.
Love all mortal woe disdains,
And in heaven its end attains ;
  There it need no foe repel ;
  " *In heaven ambition cannot dwell.*"

Time, beneath whose lasting sway
Kingdoms fall and thrones give way,
  Doth in vain to Love apply.
Malice, Vice, and Enmity,
Each must bow to Death's decree ;
  Love may all his power defy.
When the heart-beat slowly wanes,
Feelings few the soul retains,
  Only Love may go on high,
  " *With life all other passions fly.*"

Fame may fade and fall away ;
Beauty ever must decay ;
   Time doth often wealth dispel ;
Pleasure knows no constancy :
Joy will fold her robes and flee ;
   Peace may take her flight as well ;
Friendship seldom firm remains ;
Happiness but rarely reigns ;
   Care even Hope's bright beams may quell, .
   " But Love is indestructible."

FAITH AND REASON.

ONCE, in the head or the heart of man,
   Faith, a beautiful angel, dwelt ;
There was ample room within for her,
And she was a gentle comforter
   Who made him glad when at prayer he knelt;
      And his path was clear,
      For he felt no fear
As on life's race he ran.

Reason, too, had its home in his head ;
   There was plenty of room for both to thrive,
But Reason, he grew like a giant tall,
And pushed poor, trembling Faith to the wall,
   Till she pined and was scarce alive ;
      But the path of life
      Was beset with strife
When Faith was almost dead.

Yet Reason, the giant, would domineer,
   Till Faith, the angel, perished quite.
Man strove to revive poor Faith awhile,
And prayed and pined for her heavenly smile,
   For he missed her kindly light ;
      He was grieved to mark
      That his path was dark
With dread and doubt and fear.

HARMONY.

WHEN the gods from mortals parted,
    Leaving earth of good bereft,
Just to keep us hopeful-hearted
    Love and harmony were left.

Thus we hold this heavenly treasure,
    Long by hands immortal taught,
Left on earth for human pleasure
    In a moment's gracious thought.

Though from keys æolian stealing,
    Though we touch the trembling wire,
All their birth divine revealing,
    Heavenward still the strains aspire.

Though from gifted voices swelling,
    Though in organ tones they break,
All a soul's emotions telling
    Of immortal life they speak.

Greatest gift to mortals given,
    Left by those immortals here,
Thou canst waft our souls to heaven,
    Floating to thy native sphere.

ON A BLOCK OF MARBLE.

WITHIN this rugged mass of marble lies
    A statue not less fair than those which stand
Beckoning along Rome's ancient galleries,
    The work of some old master's skilful hand

Each life-like curve of feature here is hid ;
    The polished brow, slight nose, and rounded cheek,
Each ear, each sightless eye, and drooping lid,
    The inviting chin, and lips that almost speak.

All these are here, with bust and waist and hips,
    With limbs which claim our worship or our sighs ;
All here *unseen*, until the sculptor chips
    The stone away that hides them from our eyes.

THE CUCKOO.

HARK ! 'tis the cuckoo's note,
　　Across the meadows calling ;
Afar its echoes float,
　　With flute-like softness falling.

Unseen she sits and sings
　　In tones subdued and mellow,
Yet with some magic flings
　　Her voice far o'er the fallow.

Far o'er the fresh green grass,
　　The straight young wheat and clover,
The lane where the cattle pass,
　　And the brook that tumbles over.

'Tis heard where the butterfly
　　Flits o'er the hedgerow mazes,
And where to the April sky
　　The patient daisy gazes.

It comes and goes on the air
　　While the wings of the swallow glisten ;
We scarce know whence or where,
　　But we pause awhile and listen.

THE DANCER.

HER motions with the merry music blending,
　　Behold how fairy-like she foots the dance,
　　A world of witchery in her ev'ry glance
To elder hearts youth's fire and fervour lending ;
Her nimble feet, in rhythmic grace descending,
　　Patter the boards, while the bright lamps enhance
　　Her loveliness : each gazer, in a trance,
With his whole soul is ev'ry step attending.

Ah me, the power of those alluring charms !
　　Hebe herself might in such guise appear,
　　　Her lithe limbs half-revealed through gauzy dress,
Showing her slender waist and supple arms,
　　Her beauties which Old Time may never sere,
　　　And all her sweet, enduring youthfulness.

SUMMER.

Hum of insect, song of bird,
  Sigh of Zephyr blowing,
Sound of branches lightly stirred,
  Hue of roses growing ;

Scent of woodbine in the lane,
  Where the hay-cart passes,
Floral gems agleam again
  'Mid the wayside grasses ;

Shady banks that reach abroad
  Where the brook meanders,
Shadeless heat of dusty road
  Where the vagrant wanders.

Clumsy flight of butterflies
  O'er the bramble bushes,
Hidden duckling's infant cries
  'Mong the flags and rushes ;

Maze of flowers, tall and rank,
  In the unmown meadows,
Tangled foliage, green and dank,
  'Mid the woodland shadows ;

Such are part of Summer's store,
  But the store is swelling ;
These are hers and many more,
  All beyond the telling.

OMNIPOTENT MAMMON.

TRIUMPHANT yet the wide world o'er,
    The monarch Mammon rides elate ;
His votaries crowd on ev'ry shore
    To call him God and keep him great.

O'er human hearts, o'er human souls,
    He still maintains his iron sway ;
His hand the regal key controls
    That keeps the honours of a day.

He trips young Virtue by the heels, ·
    And paves the way to Falsehood's door,
And still his grinding chariot-wheels
    Are ever rolling o'er the poor.

Before him millions cringe and cower ;
    Her treasures Art to him uplifts ;
Fair Truth for him forgets her power ;
    Shrewd Science brings him all her gifts.

Supreme, omnipotent, he rules
    O'er ev'ry faction, sect, and tribe ;
By him the wise are changed to fools ;
    'Tis said, e'en Love will take his bribe.

REGAL JUNE.

By sun-kissed banks
    Of lake and mere,
The floral ranks
    More close appear.
As the regal June her largess throws
    In stintless measure where she passes ;
        On ev'ry hand
        Throughout the land
    Rich jewels glance 'mid leaves and grasses,
And a priceless wealth in the woodland grows,
    Where mated birds sing cheerily.

The year has gained
    Its fairest time,
The fields attained
    Their greenest prime,
And the verdant lanes are all agleam
    With roses smiling on the bushes ;
        The days belong
        To love and song ;
    The iris nods anear the rushes ;
The fishes flash in the winding stream,
    And the sunny days go merrily.

FAIRIES' SONG.

Over the grass in a jocund troop,
　Down the moonlit mead, we stray ;
Under the trees in a tireless troop,
　Hand in hand, till morn we play.

Gaily with wanton ease we trip
　Over the dew-wet clover beds,
Lightly we step as we dance and skip
　Over the daisies' drooping heads.

　　Round and round away we go,
　　　While the silver moonbeams play ;
　　Backward, forward, to and fro,
　　　Thus we pass the night away.

Merrily now from the band we break ;
　All in straggling troop we run ;
Under the hedgerows we hide and seek,
　All in a vein of artless fun.

Nimbly the foxgloves' stalks we climb,
　Or the slender harebells ring ;
Blithely we chant to the elfin chime,
　Or in kingcup-cradles swing.

　　Thus we spend the moonlit hours,
　　　Backward, forward, to and fro ;
　　Skipping round the sleeping flowers
　　　Till the east begins to glow.

JUNE'S ELEGY.

In the languorous dusk of a midsummer night
  We kept watch while the lovely June died,
And the stars o'er her couch shed their glimmering light,
  While in sadness we whispered and sighed.

Not a tremulous note in the underbrush stirred,
  Not a flutter of wings overhead,
Not a cry or call through the silence was heard,
  So we knew all too well she was dead.

For the night-warbling minstrel who sang at her birth,
  At her vigils no longer remained,
And a glory had gone from the ways of the earth,
  For the freshness of summer had waned.

Oh, we loved her indeed while she dwelt in her place,
  Full of beauty and loveliness rare,
And we felt a new joy as we gazed on her face,
  For we found her right royal and fair.

Long, long to our hearts will her mem'ry be dear,
  When the chillness and darkness come round ;
So we'll scatter rose petals all thick on her bier,
  And prepare her an odorous mound.

For she goes from our midst like a friend that departs,
  And her sister comes in with the morn,
But we keep not for her such a place in our hearts
  As for June in the time she was born.

A SLUMBER SONG.

OH soft wind shoreward blowing to me,
  Wafting a somnolent, restful song,
Whence have you wandered across the sea?
  Where o'er the land do you haste along?
Lightly, as over the headland you sweep,
Sing me to sleep, sing me to sleep!

While snug in this leaf-shaded hammock I lie,
  You bend the green branches above my head,
You creep through the boughs with a dreamy sigh,
  And sing to me soft till my thoughts are fled.
Oh, thus let me sleep, like a bird in its nest;
Rock me to rest, rock me to rest!

A CLOUDY DAY.

The cool wind sighs across the wheat,
  As westward down the slope it sweeps,
And, where the wood and meadow meet,
  The pheasant in its cover keeps.

Upturned against the eastern blast,
  Their under sides the light leaves show,
While mournful whispers wander past
  Along each melancholy bough.

A small bird twitters in the thorn—
  A tuneless ditty, low and brief,
And all along the lane are borne
  Faint echoes of a wordless grief.

Across the sullen, sunless sky,
  Close packed, and labouring heavily,
The vapour billows roll on high,
  Like waves upon a stormy sea.

A MAY MELODY.

OVER the May-green mead
    The scents of blossom float,
And on the fragrant air
    There falls the cuckoo's note.
The fields and trees are fair,
And the earth is glad indeed.

Gaily the floral race
    Peep from their grassy beds
With bright enamelled eyes ;
    Their many-coloured heads
Upraised toward the skies
In beauty and in grace.

Fairer than these, than all,
    Is she whose hand I take,
In the May-time of her years,
    With soul but just awake :
In the after-time of tears
This joy shall I recall.

TO A FADED PRIMROSE.

FAIR flower that bloomed beside the meadow gate,
    Thy five pale petals open to the sky,
I grieve to ponder o'er thy cruel fate,
    And find thee left to die.

Plucked by some thoughtless mortal's ruthless hand,
    To gratify a momentary whim,
Then flung aside to perish in the sand,
    Lovely no more to him ;

Thine is the lot of others no less fair,
    That, unprotected, bloom in humble ways,
And fall unwarned into the tempter's snare,
    To end in woe their days.

BALLADE OF A MODERN WITCH.

THE witches of long, long ago
   Were ugly as ugly could be,
But those whom at present we know
   Are pretty, and charming to see—
   At least, they are charming to me,
For I yield to their magical sway,
   And I own, yea, I own it with glee,
I'm bewitched by a witch of to-day.

The spell does not work me much woe,
   But it costs me some time—a dear fee,
For I follow where'er she may go,
   O'er moorland and mountain and lea ;
   Nor have I a wish to be free
From the charms that have led me astray,
   Though to such an alarming degree
I'm bewitched by a witch of to-day.

She comes not when winds wildly blow
   With shrieks that would cause me to flee,
But she comes when the sun sinketh low,
   And she whispers her love-sweet decree ;
   I meet her beneath the elm tree,
But I must not repeat what we say ;
   If you heard but the half, you'd agree
I'm bewitched by a witch of to-day.

ENVOY.

Princess, as we sail o'er life's sea,
   On the voyage near your side let me stay ;
I pray you let this be my plea—
   I'm bewitched by a witch of to-day.

A SUMMER NIGHT.

SLOWLY the evening star
  Sinks to the lingering light,
  To the portals of the night
On the horizon edge afar.

Within the vaulted skies,
  So silent, vast, and clear,
  The lesser stars appear
More bright as twilight dies.

The night her spell has thrown
  O'er all the land around,
  And now with hush profound
She reigns supreme, alone.

Not even the nightingale
  The dreamy stillness stirs
  With those sweet notes of hers
That tell the lover's tale.

Yet, wakeful till the dawn,
  Some restless souls keep watch,
  And yearn in vain to catch
The drift of things unknown.

TO THE SUN.

GREAT source of earthly life, and fount of light,
  Thou that createst and sustainest all,
  Whereon thy living beams with radiance fall,
Whence is thy fire so gloriously bright?
By day thou bring'st a thousand gems to sight,
  Paintest the flowers that Eden days recall;
  And when thou settest, like a molten ball,
The fair dead moon reflects thy rays by night.

Long shall thy gracious warmth to earth descend,
  Giving its creatures love and lust and strength,
    To generate their like, as in the past;
Yet must thy quick'ning influence have an end:
  From pole to pole the frost will creep at length,
    And death and darkness reign supreme at last.

GOOD-BYE.

(A VILLANELLE).

KISS me, Love, and say good-bye;
  Light is fading, we must part:
There are angels waiting nigh.

Only learn thou to comply,
  So shall death forget its smart;
Kiss me, Love, and say good-bye.

Life such joy did all deny;
  Haste ere death the rapture thwart;
There are angels waiting nigh.

Darling, cease to weep and sigh;
  Tears an added pang impart.
Kiss me, Love, and say good-bye.

'Tis not bitter thus to die,
  Whilst thou hold'st me to thy heart.
Kiss me, Love, and say good-bye,
There are angels waiting nigh.

SONG.

WHEN cowslips made the meadows fair,
  I met a maid of matchless charms,
And straightway loved, but did not dare
  To woo her then with hasty arms.

When days grew long and nights were fleet,
  I watched where none could hear my sighs,
And often planned the maid to meet,
  But wooed her only with mine eyes.

When summer birds were flying hence,
  I still pursued my silent quest,
With passion all the more intense,
  And wondered if my thoughts she guessed.

And now, when storms becloud the sky,
  I dread them not, though wild they be;
'Tis spring to know that she is nigh,
  'Tis summer if her face I see.

AFTER HARVEST.

THE harvest work is over,
  The sheaves are gathered in,
And ricks await their cover
  Ere stormy days begin.

Beside the dusty highway
  The stubble-fields are bare,
And down the shady byway
  The gleaners home repair.

And now the flowers are dying
  Along the sloping lea,
And songless flocks are flying
  Forlorn from tree to tree.

And birds of many a feather,
  That came ere spring was o'er,
Have gone away together
  To seek a sunnier shore.

The lanes are all forsaken
  Where children late were seen,
And riper tints have taken
  The places of the green.

By cooler breezes battered,
  The slender branches sway,
And rustling leaves are scattered
  Along the lonely way.

SONNET.

A CRYSTAL pool, reflecting half the sky,
  Lay, an unrippled mirror, on the waste;
  Its sleeping waters, taintless, clear, and chaste,
Gave only back the lucid blue on high;
But lo!—perchance its purity to try—
  A drop of oil upon the pool was placed,
  When straightway the reflection was effaced,
And o'er it spread all colours that may vie.

'Tis thus the pious mind, intent on heaven
  With rapt endeavour, steadfast and serene,
    Reflects the flawless harmony above;
But when the oil of doubt, that restless leaven
  Is dropped within, there straightway intervene
    Despair, hope, anguish, passion, grief, or love.

AT THE PARTING WAYS.

WELL, if we needs must part, so let it be;
I hold no doubt about the way I take.
'Tis rough, I know, and much beset with care,
But honours wait on those who overcome.
Nay, comrade, do not hold me back; 'tis vain,
For, see, the path lies there and I must go.
Come with me if you will; if not shake hands.
In truth, I grieve to leave you. I shall long
Remember this sad parting; oft recall
The boyhood sports we shared; dwell with regret
On the lost joys we knew; and sometimes sigh
O'er those delightful visions of our youth.
My heart will yearn to greet you as of yore,
To give its secrets for your sympathies,
And pour its new conceptions in your ear.
One course we two together long have held;
Together studied, wondered, wept, or laughed;
But now the path divides and we must part;
That way you go, I this. Farewell, farewell!

ROBERT BURNS.

O BARD beloved, whose fiery song
   Hath echoed in the hearts of men,
Who praised the right and scorned the wrong
   With ever keen and cantless pen ;

Thine was the richly-gifted soul
   That found its burden all too great
To keep within the close control
   Of others' passionless estate.

Was ever mortal tempted so,
   When Venus beckoned thee away ?
Was ever man more lured to go,
   When Bacchus led thy feet astray ?

For freedom, truth, and liberty,
   Thy voice above the rest was heard ;
And Beauty owes a debt to thee,
   But most by Love thy heart was stirred.

The pleasure that has no alloy,
   No mortal ever yet did know—
Thine were the highest heights of joy,
   And thine the deepest depths of woe.

SONNET.

As one who on a summit takes his stand,
   In sight of cities vast, but out of sound,
   And views the teeming thoroughfares around,
Where tower and spire uprise on ev'ry hand,
Beholding how the streets and squares are planned,
   How countless varied tenements abound,
   How strength and weakness side by side are found,
And how the further suburbs far expand :

So have I stood aloof and looked on life,
   While clamorous crowds were moving to and fro,
     And watched the eager concourse onward press,
But, gazing calmly on the scene of strife,
   Where joy and grief were visible below,-
     Have felt above all gladness or distress.

'

WINTER BEAUTIES.

Though harsh and wild rude Winter be,
 He surely is not all unfair,
 For, though he strips the branches bare,
He gives us pictures fair to see.

The snow transfigures lawn and lane
 In curving drifts and graceful lines,
 And oft with delicate designs
The frostwork decks the window-pane.

And, lo ! how Phœbus' sinking car
 Upthrows and spreads its golden glow,
 Like furnace fires across the snow,
Unfelt, but beautiful afar.

In sparkling raiment, white and fair,
 The leafless bushes stand revealed ;
 The springs with frost-wrought bonds are sealed,
And purple tints pervade the air.

By fairy gems and jewels decked,
 The very path is all agleam,
 And faded flags beside the stream
With frost, like dust of stars, are flecked.

The moon shines clearer through the night ;
 The stars a brighter radiance wear ;
 And now the flowerless fields appear
Arrayed in robes of spotless white.

THE INFINITE.

AMONG the countless orbs that roll through space
  Within their ordered orbits day and night,
  With changeless motion and unaltered light,
Our little earth hath its appointed place ;
Yet who of all its puny mortal race
  Can gaze into the far-off starry height
  And grasp the thought of regions infinite,
Or to the skies a boundary line can trace ?

IN MEMORIAM.

(TENNYSON).

Sorrow, avaunt !   Unveil not here thy face ;
  Reserve thy tears for those who die unblest ;
Let him be laid unwept for in his place,
  Let him, unmourned for, rest.

Thou hast no voice in such an end as this ;
  Thy part is in defeat, not victory ;
Keep all thy tears for lives that fall amiss,
  His nothing claims from thee.

Fame's lustrous halo round his name shall cling ;
  His words unto men's lips shall ever rise ;
His songs in clearest tones shall ever ring ;
  Cheering both weak and wise.

Unfaltering through all doubt his faith was borne ;
  He went his way serenely to the end ;
And even Death, of all its terrors shorn,
  Met him as friend meets friend.

A WINTER SONG.

WHEN winter winds are whistling
　　Across the naked glen,
And all the trees are bristling
　　With leafless stems again ;
When northern gales are battering
　　On shutter, wall, and door,
And laden clouds are scattering
　　Their burden to the floor ;
　　　　　Oh, then we'll keep the ingle-nook,
　　　　　　And list the stormy voices wail,
　　　　　While in some lovers' story-book
　　　　　　We read a summer tale.

When hollow sounds are rumbling
　　In chimney, porch, and hall,
And whirling flakes are tumbling
　　With soft and silent fall ;
When countless specks are glittering
　　Like diamonds of the frost,
And robin sits a-twittering
　　Upon the swollen post ;
　　　　　Oh, still we'll keep the ingle-nook,
　　　　　　And list the stormy voices wail,
　　　　　While in some lovers' story-book
　　　　　　We read a summer tale.

AN ELEGY OF TWO.

THREE loves had I on a time,
  And I thought them a dainty set ;
One was the Muse who has taught me rhyme,
And one was a maid in her fairest prime,
  The other was Violet.
  And I might have loved them yet,
Did time commit no theft ;
        But one is dead,
        Another is wed,
And but for the Muse, who alone is left,
My life of love would be all bereft.

Thus with his choicest loves
  A poet is bound to part,
As a fancier parts with his prettiest doves,
Or a titled lady her cast-off gloves,
  But it seldom breaks his heart ;
  And if it should chance to smart,
And to feel depressed and sore,
        For an hour or so
        When he sees them go,
He knows his trouble will soon be o'er,
For of younger loves there are plenty more.

BALLADE OF DECEMBER.

WITH a rush and a roar and a whirl,
　All severe in his northern array,
Here his banners he comes to unfurl,
　So to conquer and carry the day ;
　He will capture, imprison, or slay,
All the fugitive beauties of earth ;
　He will rule with tyrannical sway,
But his reign shall be ended in mirth.

All his missiles so white he will hurl
　At the creatures who come in his way,
And his snowy drift-trenches shall curl
　At the top in the thick of the fray ;
　He will bury the dead leaves away,
And the birds will lament o'er the dearth ;
　He will fill many hearts with dismay,
But his reign shall be ended in mirth.

Like a heartless and merciless churl,
　He will change ev'ry colour to grey ;
He will bluster and batter and twirl ;
　He will check ev'ry brook in its play ;
　He will drive all the sunshine astray ;
He will send all the melody forth ;
　But let him rage on as he may,
For his reign shall be ended in mirth.

ENVOY.

Prince, December may speed or delay,
　Yet its close all the waiting is worth,
He has little outside to display,
　But his reign shall be ended in mirth.

A WINTER SUNSET.

The western sky is all aflare
  With sunset fire of gorgeous hue,
While far and high a mellow glare
  Spreads upward to the blue.

Its glow pervades the lower space,
  Its light the wind-swept clouds enfold,
And far as any eye can trace
  The earth is tinged with gold.

O'erhead the sky is cold and clear,
  The evening air is crisp and keen,
And on the frosty atmosphere
  A purple tinge is seen.

Reflected from the western glow
  The east a touch of crimson wears,
While in the hazy space below
  The wan, white moon appears.

The sunset fire begins to die,
  And from the unknown space afar
There glances downward from the sky
  A solitary star.

A NEW YEAR CAROL.

O'ER vale and hill,
  Over moor and town,
O'er river and rill,
  O'er mead and down,
A joyous peal through the midnight floats,
 And to ev'ry ear its message tells.
   Ring on, ring on,
   The old year's gone ;
And afar the jubilant chorus swells,
As it falls from a thousand brazen throats,
 While the New Year bells ring merrily.

To ev'ry door
  The news is flung ;
To rich and poor,
  To old and young ;
With a glorious hope the sound is fraught,
 And echoes in tones of gladness fall.
   Ring on, ring on,
   The old year's gone ;
A burden of promise is borne to all,
 And a cadence of pleasure in ev'ry note,
For the glad New Year comes cheerily.

LOVE AND FAME.

Two maids I wooed upon a day,
　　Both rich in favours all would share:
One, Love, a laughing, winsome fay ;
　　The other, Fame, surpassing fair.

With fervour both I far pursued,
　　Nor ever thought I wooed amiss ;
But, lo ! they parted by a feud ;
　　That way went Fame, while Love took this.

Alas ! I could not cling to both ;
　　But now was come the hour to choose ;
To part from either I was loth,
　　With this to gain, and that to lose.

'Come, mortal, come with me,' said Fame,
　　With flattering voice that charmed my ear :
'The nation's tongue shall speak thy name,
　　And thou the victor's crown shalt wear.'

Love, like an angel, lingering, smiled :
　　'Ay, woo *her*, if thou wouldst,' she cried.
But Love had conquered ; like a child
　　I followed, and was satisfied.

SONNET—FOR A PICTURE.

WELL pleased am I, fair damsel, to have seen
  This sweet resemblance of thy flawless face;
  Thy snowy shoulders' rarest maiden grace;
That flower-crowned brow, where kissing fringes lean;
Those tender eyes, beyond all else serene;
  Those hallowed lips, where passion leaves no trace;
  That dainty neck, where tresses interlace;
And white-robed bust, as of a virgin queen.
When strife shall my tranquillity impair,
  And poignant sorrows fill my heart with pain,
Let me behold thy face, so sweet and fair,
  That, as I gaze into those eyes again,
  I may some inward quietude attain,
Caught from the deep soul-calm depicted there.

———

SONNET.

(ON HEARING A LITTLE GIRL SING DURING A SEVERE THUNDERSTORM.)

FRAIL child of fearless soul and steady eye,
  Who singest 'mid the thunder's ominous crash,
  And calmly views the lightning's livid flash
Dart its forked terrors down the storm-black sky;
Unmoved while battling rain-clouds burst on high,
  And land-deluging waters earthward dash;
  Amid the fierce storm's climax and the clash,
Unawed by all its awful majesty;
Thus may I stand, as fearless of all harm,
  When the black storm of Death at last draws near,
  And all its terrors compass me about,
My face as free from shadow of alarm,
  My voice as steady and my brow as clear,
    My soul as void of all despair and doubt.

THE WHITE WONDER.

Lo, what a marvel of the night
   This wondrous winter dawn beholds !
A region dazzling to the sight ;
A mantle more than marble white
   The common earth enfolds.

The magic builders of the air
   Last night a playful vigil kept ;
Each rugged angle, sharp and spare,
Was smoothed and rounded soft and fair
   And white, while yet we slept.

On ev'ry hand their art we trace,
   Their art that men have never caught,
Adorning e'en the meanest space
With softest curves of matchless grace,
   In alabaster wrought.

TO THE PRINCESS OF WALES.

THOU peerless daughter of an alien race
   Who made our island thy adopted land,
   Linking thy fortunes to our Prince's hand,
With all thy native modesty and grace,
Leaving thine own our friendships to embrace ;—
   Long have we loved thee ; still dost thou command
   Our faith and homage, and may henceforth stand
Worthiest of all to fill that honoured place.

A pattern thou for mothers high and low,
   Yet more a pattern of the patient wife ;
    A woman ev'ry nation must adore ;
Long mayest thou live to watch our empire grow,
   A peaceful angel guarding us from strife,
    A Royal Hebe, young for evermore.

A CONSOLATION.

Fair summer may hasten her flight;
  Her pleasures and glories may fade,
And the beauties in which we delight
  May vanish from garden and glade.

The chill wind may sigh in the trees,
  Fierce tempests may howl up the glen,
The swallows may haste o'er the seas,
  And the sun may but shine now and then.

But, Doris, my darling, I vow
  Thy season of beauty ne'er wanes;
Love's sunlight is still on thy brow,
  And the rose on thy cheek still remains.

On thy lips all the sweetness still lies,
  Thy touch has a charm to endear,
The love-light glows warm in thine eyes,
  And thy voice is a song in mine ear.

THE SWALLOW.

LITTLE bird with watchful eye,
  Gliding lightly o'er the meadow,
  Swifter than the dark cloud's shadow,
Whither, whither dost thou fly,
    Low and high?
      Up the lane,
      Back again,
      O'er the hedges,
      By the sedges;
Then away across the clover,
  Past the barley-field beyond,
Swooping where the brook runs over,
  Skimming o'er the shallow pond.

Other birds will sit and sing
  Through the lazy summer weather,
  But o'er fallow, grass, and heather
Thou art ever on the wing,
    Busy thing!
      Oh, to be
      Like to thee,
      Slothful never,
      Wakeful ever;
Up and stirring in the morning,
  Always earnest in the strife,
Ease and idle hours scorning,
  Making all we can of life.

THE SPIRIT OF THE SEASON.

A CHRISTMAS LYRIC.

Swiftly downward winging,
  From the regions bright,
Flies a spirit, singing,
  Through the starlit night ;
From the mystic portals
  Where the pleiads shine,
Down she comes to mortals
  Bearing gifts divine.

Every impulse tender
  To the earth she brings ;
Inspirations render
  Radiance to her wings ;
Kindliest influences
  Hover in her wake—
Banish all pretences,
  Kindness for its sake.

Stars of Christmas, gleaming,
  Light her to our land ;
Soon the spirit, beaming,
  In our midst shall stand.
Welcome gracious spirit,
  From the regions bright,
Long may earth inherit.
  Something of thy light.

.

A CHRISTMAS GREETING.

(WRITTEN FOR A CHRISTMAS CARD.)

To you I send this little token :
    A trifling gift from friend to friend ;
And with it many a wish unspoken
        To you I send.

May ev'ry Christmas blessing blend
    Around you, and may peace unbroken
Your hearth and home and heart attend.
    By ne'er a care or cross provoken
May you the festive season spend ;
    A wish sincere, let this betoken,
        To you I send.

TO W. E. GLADSTONE.

WHEN Æsop with his lamp at midday ran
    Among the Athenian thoroughfares of old,
    Where crafty Orient merchants bought and sold,
Searching in mart and temple for a *man,*
'Tis true the wise old fabulist began
    His fruitless task too early ; though so bold,
    How could he from the dross discern the gold,
Or read men's hearts, when angels scarcely can ?

Had Æsop lived to see this century wane,
    Among the clamorous millions of our earth,
    Struggling from ev'ry thraldom to be free,
He would not now have sought his man in vain ;
    But finding still his lamp of little worth,
    He would have cast it down and come to *thee.*

DAWN.

WHEN the violet arch grows pearly grey
   O'er the eastern plains afar,
When the thrush awakes to its matin lay
   By the glint of the morning star;
When dusky phantoms of the night
   Do fold their robes and flee,
And the jubilant fairies take their flight
   To their home by the green-wood tree;
When fugitive shades to the woodland rush,
   And the darkness westward flies,
The fair young Dawn with a rosy flush
   Looks up in the eastern skies.

———

WHEN HEARTS ARE YOUNG.

WHEN hearts are young and eyes are bright,
   Life's like a song in concord sung.
No care can mar its rare delight
     When hearts are young.
   Oh, sweet as honey to the tongue
Are those glad years of youthful might
   When woes unto the winds are flung.

Attended by some joyous sprite,
   The dauntless youth climbs ev'ry rung,
And days in gladness wing their flight,
     When hearts are young.

TO A WILD BEE.

MUSICAL wanderer, whence has thou come
    Over the furze and clover?
Whither away with eager hum?
    Tell me, thou restless rover.

What is that cause of thy ceaseless haste
    Over the purpling heather?
Are there such numberless cups to taste?—
    So many sweets to gather?

Where is the need of thy ardent quest?
    Are thou a false alarmist?
Wilt thou not linger, like me, to rest—
    Here, where the sun is warmest?

" All through the cold of the winter hours,
    Safe in the earth, I slumbered.
Now I must toil 'mid the scented flowers,
    For the sunny days are numbered.

" I must keep to my task with might and main
    While sunlit skies are glowing,
And then I may rest at my ease again
    When winter winds are blowing."

Thou teachest a lesson for mortals meant
    And I am fain to learn it :
To toil in haste for days ill spent,
    And ere I rest to earn it.

JUNE.

YOUNG May, the maid light-hearted,
   Who came in April's place,
Has blessed us and departed,
   The gayest of her race.

Her sister, this new-comer,
   Will win her share of praise ;
We hail her Queen of Summer,
   Who brings the longest days.

What beauty she discloses,
   As, with her wondrous art,
She brings to life the roses,
   And spreads her gems apart !

She gilds the rocky ledges,
   That lately looked forlorn ;
And 'mid the leafy hedges,
   She rears the woodbine's horn.

She lingers on the mountain,
   Her floral gifts to shower,
And drops by pool and fountain
   Full many a random flower.

In dark, unbrageous shadows,
   She bids the bluebell rise,
And o'er the flowery meadows
   She sends the butterflies.

No dearth or blight or sadness
   Unto her days are lent ;
In beauty, light, and gladness,
   Her brief career is spent.

BALLADE OF AN APRIL MORNING.

I LINGERED by the meadow gate,
    When blossoms decked the apple tree,
For Love had whispered where to wait,
    The idol of my heart to see.
    Oh, she was ev'rything to me,
Since first her sunny smile I saw,
    As blithe she rambled o'er the lea
That April morning long ago.

A skylark, soaring up elate,
    O'erwhelmed the music of a bee ;
A thrush, to cheer his patient mate,
    Sent forth a flood of melody ;
    Each living thing was filled with glee,
To feel the springtime's quickening glow,
    But none was half so glad as she,
That April morning long ago.

The daffodils, though blooming late,
    Were still as pretty as could be :
While all the glorious floral state
    Vied in a coloured company :
    Yet any critic would agree
That she more loveliness did show,
    All in her maiden majesty,
That April morning long ago.

Envoy.

Prince, this was how I met my Kate,
    Where pretty primrose clusters grow ;
And this was where I learnt my fate,
    That April morning long ago.

ROUNDEL.

If Love were nought and Mammon all,
  How hath her name such wonders wrought?
And why should Love the world control,
    If Love were nought?

True hearts by Mammon ne'er were bought:
  The gods of gold may stand or fall,
But Love that lasts must still be sought.
  Through Love our Eden we recall,
And of our lost estate are taught;
  For what could mortal care console,
    If Love were nought?

IN MARCH.

With the song of the jubilant thrush,
  With the daisy and celandine,
With buds for each wayside bush
  And a largess of shower and shine;
With the blackbird's blithesome trill,
  And the skylark's merrier lay,
With verdure for vale and hill,
  And a longer, brighter day;
With a promise of bloom and leaf,
  With the primrose in the glen,
With solace for winter's grief,
  The springtide comes again.

A COUNTRY SONG.

WHEN roses blushed upon the brier,
  Above the budding bramble,
I met a dainty country maid
  While on a morning ramble;
    A slender maid,
    A tender maid,
A maiden of the meadows.

A fair and winsome girl was she,
  Slim, graceful, and light-hearted;
So, tempted by her saucy smile,
  I kissed her ere we parted:
    A gracious kiss,
    A precious kiss,
A kiss of lasting sweetness.

Old Time will steal the joys of youth,
  And years will leave their shadows,
But I shall mind the day I met
  That maiden in the meadows;
    That slender maid,
    That tender maid,
That maid whose charms were many.

'

SONNET.

ERE baffled winter, at fair Spring's first nod,
  His weakened forces northward home hath led,
  While remnant drifts about our path are spread,
The crocus bursts the bondage of the sod ;
And, lo ! where late among the snow we trod,
  The blossom sunward lifts its dainty head,
  White, purple, gold, along the garden bed,
To catch the first warm glances of its god.

Thus, in some gloomy season of the heart,
  When sorrow all our joy hath overspread,
    And ev'ry voice seems but to make us sad,
New hopes arise ere pain can all depart ;
  We fling aside the discontent and dread,
    And go our way with faces bright and glad.

THE SIMPLER LIFE.

LET others sigh for wealth or fame,
    And at their lot repine,
Though poor in purse, unknown my name,
    A simpler wish is mine.

The doubtful pleasures men pursue
    For me were never meant ;
Give me the joys that please the few,
    And I will live content.

I crave no spacious palace home,
    Reared in some favoured spot,
Be mine the blue and sunlit dome,
    A homely, mountain cot.

I scorn to spend my precious days
    As fashion's slaves are taught ;
Give me the green, untrodden ways,
    With time and food for thought.

I shun the town's " ignoble strife ",
    The teeming street and mart,
Be mine the careless, larger life,
    The simple, joyous heart.

THE SIMPLER LIFE.—*Continued.*

Not many are the friends I own,
  Though all with smiles I greet;
I claim one kindred soul alone,
  For love and converse meet.

Though oft to melody inclined,
  New songs I seldom hear:—
The changeful music of the wind
  To me is still as dear.

And though I would not all despise
  The organ's thrilling swell;
The ocean's graver harmonies
  Shall all my gloom dispel.

———

—— FINIS. ——

www.ingramcontent.com/pod-product-compliance
Lightning Source LLC
Chambersburg PA
CBHW030024030726
47499CB00008B/3110